The Lonely Date

K. C. Carmine

THE
Lonely
DATE

K.C. CARMINE

QUEER ROMANCE
WITH HEAT

Cover design by K. C. Carmine

Image source: Canva

The people in the images are models and should not be connected to the characters in the book. Any resemblance is incidental.

Edits by: Jenn, Colin, Rebekah

Medical consultant: Teresa

Football consultant: Katie

Beta feedback: Jax

Trigger warnings: mention of attempted suicide, depression, injury, cancer. If any of these topics are triggering, please tread carefully.

Contents

Blurb

An 18k prequel story to the Blindfold Date where we get to meet Brian and Ernesto at a pivotal moment 12 years earlier as students at the same university. The Lonely Date can be read as a standalone but the HEA happens in the novel, where the two men meet again on a blind date.

Brian has always dreamt of a professional football career. Years of dedication and hard work have brought that goal within arm's reach, but now he's facing a new battle—with his sexuality he can no longer repress. Coming out—or even experimenting—would endanger his prospective career. After a devastating accident, Brian finds himself being led through doors he was reluctant to open before.

E has always struggled with intimacy. As a gay geek on the spectrum, his love life has consisted of a series of haphazard and unrewarding anonymous encounters. After a hopeless crush on a fellow student, E faces a tough decision: step out of his comfort zone and reach for what he wants, or face a life alone.

A Geek/Jock story from Pursuit of Love series - Book 1.5 This short novella can be read as a stand-alone if you haven't read the novel. Angst + steam. The MCs HEA happens in The Blindfold Date.

Manchester. Twelve years before
the events of

The Blindfold Date.

Chapter One

Ernesto

"Ernie, do you want pizza tonight?" Rod's deep voice reached E's ears as he strode into the sitting room of their tiny shared flat. The floorboards creaked under his feet, even though the worn carpet retained most of its thickness.

"Stop calling me that. I'm going to strangle Latif for telling you that stupid nickname." E sighed, smoothing his oversized hoodie as he leaned against the wall. Unfortunately, having his back to the butt-ugly damask wallpaper didn't prevent him from looking at it, as it covered all the sitting room walls. Floor-to-ceiling.

"Oh, come on, you love your brother. Besides, I only use it to rile you up." Rod chuckled, sprawling on the beaten-up sofa, his polo shirt riding up in the process. It was a welcome sight as E enjoyed his friend's complete lack of modesty, despite them never hooking up.

E rolled his eyes. "Pizza sounds great then. Will you order? I left some cash for groceries in the tea jar." He approached the mirror by the coat hangers and ruffled his hair so it wouldn't look too calm. The dark strands didn't listen, falling flat.

"Maybe I should cook something?" Rod wondered, browsing through the takeaway leaflets he'd spread on the coffee table.

"What?" E frowned. "Since when do you cook?"

"Since now, I guess." He pushed the leaflets to the side with an exasperated swipe, sending some of them to the floor. "I feel like I should lose some weight."

"Did you run into that cockhead with insults for conversation again?" E perched on the armrest of the ugly-green sofa, eyeing his friend, worry creeping up his spine.

"Maybe." Rod crossed his arms over his wide chest, then leaned back, uncrossing them. His closely-cropped beard was thick and dark and he scratched it, looking deep in thought.

"You're gorgeous and someday you'll find a man who'll love you the way you are." E leaned over, bracing an elbow on the backrest. He wished he could say the same thing when he looked into the mirror.

"Yeah, yeah. Whatever. You say all that but how come you never want to fuck me?" Rod looked at E then, his brows raised, a smirk playing at the side of his lips.

"You're too hairy for me, Rod. You know this." E punched his friend's shoulder playfully. He didn't like the texture of body hair under his fingertips, not on himself and definitely not on others. He'd only had a few lovers and always topped, but he knew what he liked by now. Or at least, what he disliked. Rod was aware of E's neurodiversity and his aversion to certain textures. He respected that in their daily routines, but good-humouredly ribbed E about the sex aspect whenever he got a chance.

"Yeah, I do," Rod grumbled. "Well, Mr Good Advice, maybe you should ditch those contacts that make your eyes water? I can tell they're bothering you." He waved a finger to indicate E's entire face. "Besides, you look good in glasses."

"No, I don't. I look like a nerd."

"I hate to break it to you, but..."

E grabbed a pillow off the sofa and hurled it at his flatmate. "At least I don't have a fringe that covers half of my face."

"It's called fashion."

"Whatever you say." The teasing air left E when he saw the expression change on Rod's face. At times like these, E regretted his tendency to say inappropriate things, unintentionally hurting others in the process. Apologising would only make it worse, he knew it from experience. Rod was hiding the burn scar above his eyebrow. Whether he thought it marred his face or he didn't want to see the reminder of whatever had happened in the mirror, E wasn't sure. The man never talked about it and E wouldn't pry.

"You're all decked out in the biggest hoodie you own and the tightest jeans the world has ever seen," Rod said, moving the subject back to E. "Are you going to watch Mr Hottie McHotness play again?"

"He has a name," E scoffed, pushing off the wall up to pace the grey carpet.

"Yeah, but he doesn't even *know* yours."

"It doesn't matter."

"You'll have to show me what he looks like someday, so I can judge your taste in men. Besides, you know guys like him don't notice guys like us, right?"

"I don't care, Rod. I just want to watch the game." E reached into the pocket of his hoodie to fiddle with the piece of paper in it. He could picture the neatly folded square clearly in his mind.

"And him."

"So what?" E shrugged, looking through the window at fellow students returning from classes. Their easy gait and laughter showed how relaxed they were around other people in public. Something that was an unreachable goal for E.

"Nothing. Just... be careful." Worry creased Rod's brow. The one not hidden behind his fringe.

"Yes, Mum." E pulled the face of a petulant child, the same one his Mum used to scold him for when he was younger.

Rod rolled his eyes. "If those stupid arseholes push you around, I'm not helping you bandage your ribs again."

E felt a shadow pain tightening his chest at the memory of that experience. The team had lost that day and the psycho-fans had been looking for anything and anyone to let their anger out on. E had been an easy target; a skinny bloke in nerdy glasses, looking out of place. "That was after a Manchester United game, not a local one," he said, downplaying how that event still haunted him.

"Yeah, whatever. You're studying computer science, you'll never use all that game knowledge for anything."

"I don't need to. I just like watching." He tried to push the glasses on his nose but they weren't there. Annoyed, he shoved his hands into the pockets of his hoodie. "A bunch of easy-on-the-eyes men running around. What's not to like?" E grabbed his rucksack off the floor and tossed it over his shoulder. The snicker of his flatmate followed him to the door until he left the flat.

In truth, watching the matches reminded him of the times he'd attended them with his family when he was little. Dad and he had been invested in the games themselves, Mum would come as snack support, and his older brother, Latif, had sat disinterested, making plaits in Mum's hair. Despite disliking crowds, E had always enjoyed family outings.

The tradition of watching sweaty guys kick a ball brought him a sense of stability, even when he was far from his home in London. Sometimes he walked the 45 minutes, an exact 2.4 miles from the uni's Kilburn Building to the sports centre. But this time, he took the 10-minute drive in his beaten-up Beetle to the gym and sports centre in the middle of UCFB's Etihad Campus in East Manchester.

The local FA practice had only a handful of people attending, sitting on the benches, some on the grass outside the field. The grounds of the sports centre were a far cry from a professional football stadium.

The upside of getting the centre's membership was having access to the indoor swimming pool as well as the gym. E had begun using the treadmills very early in the morning or late at night when no one was there. He hated people looking at his skinny frame and snickering, but he liked the feeling of utter exhaustion afterwards. It helped calm his racing mind and let him sleep better. At first, he'd come once a week, but now he made it his routine three mornings a week as his lecture's timetable allowed.

Once he'd arrived at the centre, he sat on the hood of his car, right outside of the high fence surrounding the pitch, one of three next to each other. The names of the players didn't matter, but number eleven was definitely his favourite for his moves that looked effortless, his team spirit, and his radiant smile. E took out his notebook full of scribbles from previous games and hoped that to anyone passing by, he looked like he was doing schoolwork after a workout.

The players jogged from the centre's building and onto the pitch, warming up before the match started. E jotted down possible strategies and note-worthy moments to later analyse how they could have been improved. He loved breaking down a game to its basic components. It was like writing in C++ code—he could imagine arranging the players in certain positions and gauging what could happen next, whether it was a pro game or some students running on the field. Involuntarily, he focused on Brian Withshaw, number eleven. Brian played like a pro as usual. Not only was he a team player, showing how others could rely on him, he was also a goal-scoring force of nature. It made E wonder why he hadn't been scouted yet. After each successful play, he'd wave to the girls whooping and cheering at the opposite side of the fence from E.

Seven pages of notes later, the match concluded and the players jogged off the field. Several of the men shed their shirts, number eleven among them. He revealed his perfectly honed chest, gleaming with sweat, the muscles of his arms flexing as he ruffled the blond waves that curled at his nape.

E followed him with his gaze, noticing how a small dusting of hair on his abdomen trailed down, disappearing into his shorts. The players were heading towards the centre's building, passing by the car park E was sitting at. He was still watching Brian's muscles flex, then roamed up the man's chest to his face.

He froze.

Brian's gaze was on him. He stopped in his tracks, his eyes boring into E's with his brows furrowed.

E hated eye contact in general, but he was so shocked by the green pools locking on his that he couldn't look away. He felt his face heat up. His heart pounded into his throat.

The single second felt like minutes, but soon Brian turned to his mates to laugh at something one of them said.

E sat motionless for a moment longer before his heartbeat returned to normal. He'd hoped to use the treadmill at the centre, but now he didn't want to risk bumping into the players lest he froze and made a fool of himself again.

Soaking in the June afternoon sun, a rare treat in rainy England, E closed his eyes and laid back on the hood of his tiny car, his legs dangling off the front of it. As he analysed the game in his head, his thoughts kept drifting to Brian, his smile, his blond waves bouncing as he ran on the field, his heaving chest that begged to be touched, his powerful thighs and shapely calves.

E took a deep breath but it didn't help his mind conjuring up an image of Brian in the sports centre's showers right now, naked under the spray, the water cascading down his toned body.

Shaking his head, he opened his eyes to see the car park was empty. He squeezed his gangly legs into the car and drove the short distance to park in front of his block of flats. He didn't feel like going home yet. Hefting his rucksack up, he let his feet carry him for an aimless walk.

Manchester was far different from the bustle of London he'd grown up in, and E both loved and hated it. As he walked along a row of shops, the grey buildings hosting them remembered better days, their facade, like the city itself, looked sad on the outside but held lively parties and an array of unique people. Like the ones passing E now, dressed for a Friday evening in colourful attire or smart casual, depending on their destination. E took in the city he'd grown fond of, with all its rusty signs, saggy awnings, and tired old pubs.

A ruckus of low laughter made him turn around.

The footballers, along with their friends, were heading his way. The band's incessant chatter was punctuated with raucous laughter, jarring E with its volume. It was a reminder that E didn't have a group of friends to go out Friday night with, and even if he had, he would probably be too overwhelmed to spend hours crowded by people who would never understand him. Looking ahead, he saw a local pub, realising that's where the football entourage must be heading. He tensed. He didn't want them passing by him.

Too close.

Too loud.

Too uncomfortable.

His breathing sped up, and he opened the first shop door he could reach to hide inside. The heavy door squeaked as the bell above chimed, putting him on the spot as he tumbled in. He swivelled on his heel to face the shopkeeper with heavy eyeliner and a bored expression. Her black hair fell on her shoulders and was so straight, it looked like long needles, matching the safety pins that were artisti-cally positioned along her shirt's sleeve.

Compared to the sunlight outside, the shop was bathed in darkness, bar the neon lights illuminating the shelves.

Are those... dildos?

E's gaze turned back to the shopkeeper. She eyed him with a dubious glance as she popped her pink gum, splattering it over her black-painted lips. "You alright? Can I help you?"

E looked to the door, the chatter of the footballers still behind it, then back to the dildos, looming in the purple light. "I'm just here to look around."

She waved a hand in the direction of the shop, then returned her eyes to the manga she was reading on the counter.

E took in the array of toys on display, some of which he was familiar with. He had played with his arse using his fingers and had a tiny dildo in his bedside table, but these were something else. Different shapes and sizes of silicone: from a tiny plug, to a forearm ending with fingers poised in an arrow. The view made his sphincter clench but his cock stir. It was nothing he'd want done to him, but he wouldn't mind doing it to someone else. He stepped closer to the shelf with cock-shaped dildos that stood proudly upright on their flat bases. Tilting his head, E inspected the silicone veins on each one, and the smooth edges of the glans.

A man roughly his age, dressed in ripped black jeans, was restocking the bottom shelf, straightening several items, replacing the others.

"Do they come in different colours?" E pointed to the shelf he'd been eyeing.

The man lifted himself from the crouch and shrugged. "Just beige and black. What else do you want?"

"Nothing, just asking." E looked away, his fingers playing with the folded piece of paper in the pocket of his hoodie. He focused on the labels under the toys, reading the sizes and descriptions under those which warranted one.

A prostate massager dildo caught his attention. Battery-powered. *Hmm, not very efficient.* And fucking expensive.

"This one's worth the price, I'm telling you." The restocking guy let out a low whistle and shook his head. "Yeah."

"Oh, really?" E squinted at the smooth, black toy.

"It'll blow your socks off." The guy chuckled. "It totally did mine."

Oh.

The glowing recommendation made E calculate the upcoming expenses in his head. If he wrote two, no, three more papers for other students this week, he could cover the cost. Grateful for his source of income thanks to loaded students who preferred to party rather than study, E smiled. "I'll take one."

"Good choice." The guy reached into a cupboard underneath the shelves and retrieved a black box. "Kat at the checkout will sort your payment."

"Ta for the help."

"Anytime."

Did he just wink?

E smiled in return, marched to the counter and placed the box on it.

"Not only looking around after all?" The girl, Kat apparently, pushed her manga aside to scan the box.

"Apparently not," E said, feeling a lot less embarrassed than he'd expected to be in a sex shop. The staff were laid-back and gave out an air of openness and tolerance that put him at ease.

"Would you be interested in a toy cleaner or lubricant?"

"Yeah, both. I'll take both."

He left with a black shopping bag in his backpack and anticipation in his abdomen. A cool evening breeze along with the stench of exhaust fumes hit his face as he stepped on the pavement. The pub nearby was loud with the footballers and their entourage, as well as the regular evening crowd. E left it behind as he headed to his flat, manoeuvring between the random strangers that littered the street.

Chapter Two

Brian

The scent of freshly-cut grass filled Brian's nose as he ran onto the sports centre's field alongside his mates. He felt the camaraderie in the air even as they stretched before the game—between his team and their opponents, preparing their muscles for a solid workout. This was the last practice they'd have before several of them, Brian included, would take part in the UK football trials the following week. There, he'd be able to play in front of football scouts with connections to leading clubs.

He hoped it was time for his dreams to come true, and for him to play for a professional league. All he needed was a chance to prove that he was cut out for the field. He was eager to learn and determined to work hard. Fame and money weren't driving factors for him, but the idea of buying a house each for his parents, sister, and brother held its own appeal.

At an early age he'd joined the Sunday football league, then the moment he'd moved to Manchester, he'd signed up for the local FA, hoping to pursue his passion. When it came time for uni, despite his love of architecture, he'd applied to UCFB to study football coaching and management. After one term, however, he'd realised that as much as kicking the ball was his dream, coaching wasn't. Back then, at nineteen, he'd hoped to be scouted in a trial he'd prepared to take part in, but sprained his ankle during the match before. He'd been aware that he'd recover but missed a shot at a career at what he'd thought was the perfect moment in his life. He'd been ready; in perfect shape mentally and physically, only to be hauled to the A&E mere days before he got a chance to show his talent in front of the scouts.

His parents had pleaded with him to pursue both of his dreams—architecture and football—at the same time. After the injury, he'd finally yielded and took up studying architecture at the University of Manchester while still playing ball any moment he got.

The PFSA Football Trials he'd be attending next week, at the ripe age of 22, could give him a chance to keep architecture as a hobby and let football become his full-time profession.

Now, he rolled his shoulders and looked at his mates, some of whom would probably be scouted soon. Hopefully, he would be as well. When the coach gave the signal to start, Brian's team and their opponents ran onto the field. The air of teamwork, the wind in his hair as it flapped on his forehead, and the sheer joy that playing gave him were the things that drove Brian to be the absolute best he could.

The game was a success, his team winning 3:2. Despite the fierce competition on the field, they all headed to the centre to shower with only several friendly verbal jabs in the air. Brian greeted his friends, who were waiting and cheering for him outside of the field, but a figure sitting on the hood of a Beetle by the fence momentarily distracted him.

He paused, drawn to the man with the sun setting at his back. The slight breeze blew through the man's dark hair, cropped shorter at the back. The orange and red hues around him created a surreal view, like the psychedelic cover of a vinyl album from the '70s.

Brian's eyes watered from the glow and he squinted, focusing on the man's features. He was roughly

Brian's age, probably younger judging by the sharp angles of his face.

Their eyes met and Brian could have sworn the man looked right through him and into his soul, seeing things Brian didn't even know existed. The intensity of the man's gaze was like a fiery brand to Brian's chest, burning with its permanence. A shiver ran down his spine, but in a split second, the stranger's haunting eyes turned away.

"Right, Withshaw?" A jab to Brian's side brought him back to reality. He shook out of his trance and laughed at whatever James had said as his teammate and friend led their group inside the building. Brian had the urge to look around and glimpse the young man again. Instead, he followed James, leaving the rest of their friends to meet later after the team had showered and got ready to party.

Within an hour, Brian was at the local pub, cooling his throat with a gulp of lager. Despite the heatwave, as the UK was prone to calling any weather above 25°C, they all sat closely at the pub's round tables outside. Several local elders still lingered, but the place was slowly being overtaken by residents of the nearby student housing blocks.

A swarm of pretty girls in short skirts and high heels meandered towards them with a confident gait. All their faces were familiar, but one tall beauty's smile was especially dear to Brian. A moment later, he welcomed the weight of Alice's body on his lap as she wrapped her arm around his neck. Her delicate, flowery perfume, the epitome of spring, reminded him of their nights together—exciting in their novelty and hot as hell.

Neither of them was ready to commit at this point in their lives, so their relationship had been based solely on sex. Alice wanted to experiment, to remain free and sample what the world had to offer, and Brian was hoping to get drafted. If he was given a chance to go pro after the trials, there would be no place for a relationship in his life for at least several years. Besides, as much as he enjoyed their bedroom play, he couldn't picture himself settling down with her or anyone else at this point.

Alice wiggled her cute bum, willing Brian's cock to harden in his shorts. She knew exactly what she was doing as she offered him a coy smirk. Her blond hair fell to her mid-back and she tossed it to the side, exposing her long neck and bare shoulders with only the thin strap of her blue dress interrupting the display of smooth skin.

Brian liked the attention he'd been getting from her and some of the other girls. If Alice wanted his body only, he was in no position to complain. It was easier that way for everyone involved.

Brian wrapped his arm around her waist, letting his palm rest on her hip.

"You were awesome tonight." Alice's face was close enough for him to hear over everyone's chatter.

"Thanks." Brian smiled before accepting a chip Alice fed him from his plate. Her delicate fingers reached for another one before she leaned in.

"Leave the door to your room open tonight," she whispered into his ear, then traced his earlobe with her wicked tongue.

Brian nodded, pulling her closer as anticipation filled his abdomen. "What time?"

"Nine. Be ready."

Oh fuck yeah.

The day was great so far and would get better with the evening Alice had surely already planned in detail.

That evening, Brian lay in bed on the fresh sheets he'd just changed. He'd showered, brushed his teeth, and trimmed his pubes in preparation for Alice's visit. His stereo played *Shout at the Devil* by

Mötley Crüe, but he'd switch it to something more mellow once Alice arrived.

It was past ten and he was getting bored waiting so he reached for a sports magazine on his nightstand to kill some time. Absent-mindedly, he flipped through several articles as his eyes scanned the pictures of fit footballers. The new rising star was a bloke he'd been in the Sunday league with years before. He was grown up now, holding a football in his outstretched hand, his biceps flexing, his bare chest tight with lean muscle.

Ping!

Brian tossed the magazine aside to reach for his phone.

It was Alice.

Mary's not feeling well. I can't come tonight. But I will tomorrow. Promise!

Disappointment flooded him as he texted back a polite message of condolence, despite feeling miffed that his evening was now ruined. With the heel of his palm, he willed his hard-on to stay down but it was futile. He was not getting lucky tonight. Yet, he was still horny and had to do something about it.

Alice was the only girl who'd ever played with his balls, massaging her fingers behind them, nearly to his anus. He'd always found it exhilarating, and she knew that by the wicked grin she always wore during their bedroom shenanigans. He reciprocated the sentiment and followed the detailed instructions she'd give him, whether it was how to eat her out or how much lube he had to add for anal. She'd offered to play with his arse more than once, but he'd laughed at the idea.

Straight guys don't do that. Right?

But since that night, he'd been unable to stop thinking about it. In fact, he'd been hoping today she'd offer to do it again and this time maybe he wouldn't chicken out.

Just now, only reminiscing, he was tweaking his nipple, his bare chest arching at the sweet zing the touch brought. His other hand drifted down his chest and into his boxers. He stroked his erection just once before reaching further, behind his balls to his crack. His heart beat with the drums of the music in the room: energetic, loud, and defiant. With his middle finger he grazed his pucker, the skin there like a live wire. Heat rushed to his cheeks, and he snatched his hand away.

I can't do it. I shouldn't do it.

With a grunt of frustration, Brian linked his hands behind his head and looked at the cracks in the white ceiling. Needing to focus on something else, he thought of the game today, of how well they'd played and how much he hoped his trials next week would propel his life further into football. He worked great with his team, but if he had a chance to play with professionals, he knew he'd be able to learn so much more. He recalled the rush of a successful game as he'd jogged off the field today, his legs tired, his body elated with the workout.

Then he remembered a deep brown gaze locking on him as he was leaving the field. Some guy sitting on the hood of a car. Brian had seen him before, scribbling notes, probably writing a paper right after gym time.

Today had been different.

Brian had felt those intense eyes on him like a lover's caress. It was as if the guy could sense the tiny seed of doubt Brian had about his sexuality. In a different world, at a different time, Brian could hold that gaze, could challenge it, and maybe even find out something about himself in the process.

But he wasn't in a place in his life to explore that side of him. A side he wasn't even sure he had. What would his teammates think if he'd told them he was attracted to men? Not as a casual remark, but on a serious note. Would they treat him differently? Avoid him in the locker room? Make jokes? Then he thought of the scouts, afraid of a potential scandal if he came out at an early stage of his career. He couldn't do that to himself, especially not knowing if he even was anything other than straight.

Beatrice, his older sister and the person he'd always looked up to, had always told him to be himself, to embrace who he truly was, but some things had to wait or maybe stay locked away forever.

Beatrice had come out as a teen, waving rainbow flags, piercing her nose and surrounding herself with friends who understood her. Their parents were supportive of her, so Brian wouldn't have to worry about their reaction. But he didn't have the courage his sister had, or even the guts to consider if he needed it.

He'd only ever been with girls. Sure, he'd ogled a well-built man here and there, but he was working out and into sports, there was nothing unusual about looking at other blokes' honed bodies.

Right?

He wasn't sure. It had been his first term at uni when he'd seen two guys kissing at a party for the first time. He'd seen gay couples before, amongst Beatrice's friends and other people around him, but he'd never seen such a passionate kiss up close. It had turned him the fuck on. He'd blamed it on being drunk and horny, but that image had stayed with him for years, buried somewhere at the back of his mind. He'd never thought he might want the same. With a man.

Because he didn't.

So what if he fancied a bit of experimental arse-play? It meant nothing.

His gaze followed the crack in the ceiling all the way to the door leading to the flat he shared with two other guys. They weren't home now. Probably partying and getting laid. Unlike him. Alice wouldn't come to him tonight. Wouldn't suck him off, wouldn't play with his balls, wouldn't reach behind them...

He glanced at the lube, tissues, and condoms he'd prepared on his bedside table, then back to his cock.

Yup, still hard.

Sliding his boxers down with one hand, he reached for the lube with the other. The squelching sound the bottle made as it unloaded onto his hand was loud enough for him to be glad that he was home alone. Anyone would have known what he was about to do.

He palmed his cock and released a groan, the faux-strawberry scent of the lubricant invading his nose, reminding him that it was Alice who'd brought it one night for anal play. The last song of the album finished and silence fell, making the slick sound lewd in the dead of night as he thrust into his fist, spreading his bent legs for a better angle.

Not enough.

His other hand reached for his balls and he rolled them in his palm before squeezing until a groan tore out of his throat. His fingers inched further until he grazed his puckered hole. He exhaled a breath, stilling the hand on his cock.

'Relax. It's fine,' he assured himself. 'You do this every day when you take a shower.'

But this was different. His fingers weren't quick and efficient, but probing and curious. Closing his eyes, he focused on the sensation of his pucker constricting as he circled it with the pad of a finger.

His heart pounded.

His face heated.

A trickle of lube made its way to his new point of curiosity, and he pressed with his index finger. His quick, shallow breaths punched the air as he was trying to relax his anal muscles. Finally, the tip slipped in and his lips formed a shocked 'O.'

"Oh, fuck..." he groaned on a long exhale. It was a small stretch, yet felt huge in girth and sensation alike. As if some new nerve endings had woken up and sent signals to his brain asking for more.

He pushed further.

A burning sensation fired in his anus and he pulled his finger out.

"Stupid idea," he mumbled, clenching at the mild pain.

Sitting up, he reached for the bedside table. Pulling several tissues out, he wiped his hands and tossed them into the basket by his tiny desk. Among his failed sketches, the wad of tissues didn't look all that suspicious. With a sharp tug, he pulled his boxers up.

He was being ridiculous.

He hadn't known what to expect. The burn was not it. It was probably why Alice insisted on him nearly bathing her arse in the stuff before his cock got anywhere near it.

Fuck, he didn't know what he was doing.

His eyes landed on the laptop on the desk. *Hmm.*

Not wanting to get lube on the chair, he grabbed the laptop and placed it on the foot of the bed. Lifting the lid, he woke it up, waited several moments, then opened the browser. Just as he was about to type his search, he remembered something one of his mates told him about being careful with what he looked up online. Hovering over the VPN button, he clicked it to make his search non-traceable before he typed in gay porn.

Sites started to load, along with pictures and videos. He scrolled tentatively, leaning over, his face inches from the screen.

Men dressed in leather. Fetish. Spanking.

Scroll.

A video caption of a guy in skimpy underwear with straps under his arsecheeks and fabric that covered only his junk. His football trainers were firmly planted on the locker room floor but his hands were splayed on a bench, showing his lean-ly-muscled body, similar to Brian's, that shone with sweat. He could be one of his mates.

Brian clicked on the video.

The guy was rocking his hips, arse up, his stance widening. A big, muscled man entered the frame, a gym bottle in his hand. He poured a solid amount of its contents over the bent-over guy's hole and Brian realised the bottle was filled with lube. The big man drenched his entire palm in the gooey gel as well, then unceremoniously slid three fingers into the other man, then four.

"Whoa..." Brian breathed, his eyes going wide as he clenched his arse-cheeks in sympathy.

"Open for my fist, my little slut."

Brian closed the laptop with a slap.

Nope.

Nuh-uh.

He nudged the device away with his foot, but the image was too clear in his mind to disappear so quickly. Sex with people was great. Experimenting, potentially even with guys, sounded exciting.

Porn was *weird*.

He was aware that, like everything on the telly and online, it had to be exaggerated to sell. But Brian wanted the real deal. He'd rather try new things with people than do online research. No arse play for him. No way. Not that kind. *Ouch.*

He sprang off the bed and stomped barefoot to the shared bathroom in the corridor. He locked the door behind himself with a loud click. The sticky lino was unpleasant under his feet so he kicked off his boxers, hopped into the tub, and dragged the shower curtain closed with an angry tug. Cold water should douse his crazy ideas. Horny and frustrated were not a good combination.

Brian looked down at his cock, at the tip peeking from under his foreskin, and the precome leaking on his thigh. "Stubborn," he mumbled, then turned on the shower and didn't wait for the warm water, just stepped under it. The cold spray, like tiny needles, doused his nape and his back, but the need for sexual release remained.

Palming his cock, he stroked it with quick, practised movements. Arousal built quickly in him but he wanted something different.

"Fuck it." He was no quitter.

Cursing under his breath, he turned the water off, lifted one leg on the side of the tub and reached around. The moment he touched his pucker, electricity made of pure excitement flowed through him. Heat coiled in his abdomen. Brian teased the rim with his finger, wishing he hadn't left the lube in the bedroom. There was some of it still left from his earlier attempt but probably not enough.

He pushed the tip in and moaned loudly as it disappeared into his body. It burned a little, but that heightened the intensity of the touch all the more for it. *How can this be so intense?* In a little more.

It burned so fucking bad but the stretch was too titillating for him to stop this time. He needed more. *Yes.*

He looked around frantically and reached for the bottle of conditioner. It must have been John's, he probably needed it for his long hair. Brian's hands shook with excitement as he poured some white goo on his palm and reached around again.

He aligned two fingers and rocked his arse back.

His strangled, guttural moan echoed in the bathroom before it turned into a wail as his digits sunk deeper. The bliss of the stretch made him nearly lose his balance on the slippery surface of the tub, now splattered with blobs of conditioner. He rested his head on the tiled wall and pumped his fingers. In and out.

So good.

Brian's head reeled as he let himself focus on the pleasure and not how he was getting it. Fisting his cock, he stroked and moved his fingers at the same time. His body was one mass of trembling heat, every nerve ending sensitive. His eyes squeezed shut as his ragged breathing grew quick and shallow.

Faster. Deeper. Fuller.

Almost there.

What if those were another man's fingers inside him? What if someone who understood what his body needed did that to him? Someone who could truly see him. Like the guy outside of the football field. With a penetrating gaze and lean fingers.

Brian's body went rigid, his muscles tensing before he released a groan. Eyes blown wide, he exploded, sending spurts of come on the tiled wall and tub. Barely coordinating his movements, he slid his fingers out, causing one more burst of spunk to leave him, then another.

He came so hard, his knees buckled, and his muscles went limp. Grappling for purchase, he gripped the shower curtain and dragged it with him. The plastic curtain rings broke in the process, sending pieces flying right and left as he slid into the tub.

Chapter Three

Ernesto

The door creaked when E burst into his flat and sprang past Rod, making a beeline to his room to hide his new purchases in the wardrobe.

"Everything okay, mate?" Rod's voice sounded worried.

"Yeah, fine." E shut the door and returned to the sitting room where his friend was standing in front of the mirror, its chipped frame a reminder that it was already there when they'd moved in. It was probably in this house since the nineties judging by the sparkly ornaments still stuck to it.

"How did the game go?" Rod tucked in his polo shirt, only to tug it out sharply a moment later.

"Fine. It was just another game." E lied, remembering how Brian's gaze met his, setting his entire being on fire in a single second. He swallowed and tried to settle his face into what he hoped was a neutral expression, as Rod could see his reflection in the mirror. "Then I went for a stroll." *And bought a vibrator.*

Rod narrowed his eyes but nodded as if he suspected something but didn't want to pry. Which was very unlike him. *Is he hiding something? Is he nervous? Why?*

"How do I look?" Rod straightened his back and shoved his hands into the pockets of his jeans.

E took in Rod's neatly-pressed black polo shirt and black jeans tucked into combat boots. "Like yourself."

"Wow, thanks." Rod glared over his shoulder. "I mean, do I look presentable?"

"Yeah, these jeans highlight your arse." E looked his friend up and down again, then added: "And your thick thighs."

"Sod off, Ernie!"

"What? That's a good thing!"

Rod only grumbled something under his breath as he smoothed the polo over his belly.

E didn't understand Rod's complaining about his weight or build. He was a tall, hairy guy that wasn't skinny. Unlike E, who could use more hours at the gym to look twenty and not even younger than he actually was. He'd rather look like Rod; no one asked him for ID when they went out for drinks.

"Are you going on a date?" It just occurred to E why Rod looked so fidgety.

"Not really. It's hard to explain." Rod turned around and leaned against the ugly beige wall.

"Should I be worried?" E propped his buttcheek on the armrest of the sofa, balancing his weight.

"No," Rod said, crossing his arms over his wide chest. "He's more of a mentor than a lover, although..." He let his voice trail off as he bit his lip, mischief sparkling in his eyes.

Well, this is interesting.

"You're hoping for something to happen between you two?"

"If it goes well, I'll spill the tea when I'm back. I promise."

E recalled his mother using the phrase often and it helped to decipher what his friend had in mind. "Go, get him then. I'm looking forward to a night in. I'm knackered."

"If you watch the new Merlin episode without me," Rod pointed an accusatory finger at E, "I'm not speaking to you for a week."

E lifted his hands up in surrender, chuckling. "I won't."

"Do you think we'll get to see Authur and Merlin fuck?" Rod dropped to one knee, tightening the laces on his mid-calf boots.

"On the BBC?" E laughed, "You're insane if you think they'd ever allow that."

"Oh, well," Rod shrugged. "Fanfic it is."

"Dork."

"Takes one to know one."

With that, Rod sauntered out the door, his wide shoulders nearly filling the doorframe. E hoped his roommate would get some action tonight, just like he was about to.

E patted his wet hair with a towel on his way to his room. There, in the middle of his bedspread lay a slick piece of silicone, like a trophy waiting to be admired. He'd cleaned it with the spray he'd bought and left it to dry on the bed before he'd gone to shower. He'd washed so thoroughly that his cock was at half-mast already. The sight of the beauty he'd brought home only made it harder.

Sitting cross-legged on the bed in the room he called 'a box' because of how tiny it was, E traced a finger along the shaft of the dildo, then picked it up. The silicone was smooth, without the rubbery feel he'd feared. It was heavy in his hand as he'd already put batteries in, making sure they were brand new, not from the remote, like the last time. Having a vibrator die when you're about to come was the stuff of nightmares. The manual still lay on the edge of the bed so E threw the little booklet into the top drawer of his bedside table. He'd read it already.

The instructions were very straightforward, but one could never be too careful.

The knot in his abdomen was half-excitement and half-dread of a new experience. Even one as trivial as using a toy in the quiet and comfort of his own room.

Tossing the vibrator back on the bed, he looked into the mirror on his wooden wardrobe right in front of him. He loved to watch himself when he wanked, observing his hand working and the weird expressions on his face. Now, he felt like an idiot, arranging his Friday night plans around a sex toy. Maybe someday, he could have plans with someone who would be his partner in life and in bed.

The thought brought him back to the sports centre and the game he'd witnessed earlier in the day. He laid back and closed his eyes, just like he had then when the setting sun warmed his face.

An image of Brian heading to the showers after the practice filled his mind. The water cascading down his body would wash off the sweat he dutifully earned on the field. With soapy hands, Brian would lather his honed chest and abs before washing his balls, his penis, his crack, lingering for just a moment longer than necessary.

E's cock hardened at his vivid imagination painting gorgeous pictures. He groaned, wrapping his fingers around his hard-on, pulling his foreskin down to stroke in a languid motion.

E watched Brian walk into the empty locker room to find E standing in the middle of it. E had gotten lost in the centre after his workout and wandered in. Yes, that was a good enough explanation. *Brian didn't ask questions. His eyes blazing with lust, his chest gleaming with droplets of water, he simply walked right to E and cupped his face.*

E's lips parted to explain but no words came out. Brian didn't laugh at him, didn't mock him. No, there was only heat in his gaze as he let the towel around his hips drop to the floor. There was no need for Brian to speak, 'cause after all, what would they even talk about? They probably had nothing in common. Even E's fascination with football was not the same as Brian's. But that was not important now.

Brian was in front of him, his cock bare, hard and pointing at E.

"Kiss me," E said.

Despite knowing that he hated other people's saliva, E allowed himself this fantasy. Besides, it was Brian, the golden boy.

Brian leaned over and offered E a closed-lip peck. Yes, that was what he needed. *Then he grabbed E's hoodie and lifted it up and off, ruffling E's dark-brown strands in the process.*

E's eyes focused on Brian's lips, then his tongue darting out in a languorous, erotic lick.

Guided by the overwhelming need to touch, E reached to stroke Brian's nipples with his thumbs, making the man moan for him. At the same time, Brian's hands worked E's jeans open to pull them down along with his boxers, sending goosebumps along E's legs. Grazing E's calves, Brian nudged him to step out of the clothes before straightening up. Their near-nonexistent height difference meant their breath mingled.

"Touch me." E didn't have to say it twice. The next moment his cock was in Brian's hand, the feel of his warm fist making him arch. His strokes were slow, but his grip tight, just the way E liked it.

As if knowing that E was not a fan of messy kisses, Brian latched onto E's neck, sucking and licking, before he bit his earlobe. E moaned as a full-body shiver overtook his body. A wicked grin graced Brian's handsome face when he pulled away, then dropped to kneel on the fallen towel.

E wanted to fuck this Greek-God of a man so badly, but even in his most ridiculous fantasies, he knew that was too far-fetched. *With effortless grace, Fantasy-Brian took E's cock halfway into his mouth and sucked, gently at first, then speeding up.*

E lifted his left leg to brace his foot on the near-by bench. Brian didn't protest when E tugged him away by his silky hair, watching saliva drip from his chin. As per E's imagination, Brian knew ex-

actly what E wanted and he spat on his fingers to reach E's hole.

In the present, E grabbed the newly-bought lube and squirted a dollop on his hand, letting it drip to the sheets. He'd worry about the clean-up later. Feet firmly on the bed, he spread his knees. The arousal flooding his system prompted him to act quickly, applying lube to his pucker. One finger went in, then another. E hissed at the burn, but inched further, stretching himself, imagining those were Brian's fingers. Brian was a good boy with a face of innocence, and he would follow E's instructions, he would prepare him just right.

Pulling out on a groan, E slathered a copious amount of lube on the toy. The mirror on the wardrobe showcased his lewd position: legs parted, his empty hole twitching for attention.

Holding his balls up with one hand, he positioned the vibrator with the other. He pushed out on an exhale and the tip popped in. *Oh, the glorious stretch.*

A groany-wail left him and he bit his lip so hard he tasted copper on his tongue.

Thank fuck Rod wasn't home, E didn't need to remain mortified for the rest of uni in front of his flatmate.

While he took several breaths, he reached for a pillow to put under his head so he could see himself in the mirror without straining. Bearing down, he pushed the toy in, watching as it slid further into him, out an inch, then in again, until only the base was visible. He wished someday he could find someone who'd want to spread themselves for him like that, trust E enough so he could let his imagination loose. To have his cock as deep inside someone as the vibrator was in him right now, grazing his prostate with a specially designed tip.

The deliciously full feeling drove him insane with lust, yet the idea of someone fucking him didn't appeal to him. Unless it was solely for a fantasy to get off.

His sexual experience so far had consisted entirely of awkward groping and lukewarm orgasms in the bathroom stall of a nearby gay club. His cock in a random bloke's arse until both of them came as quickly as possible in order to re-join the sweaty crowd. The nastiness of the surroundings had put E off so much, he'd been unable to truly enjoy the sex.

Alone, he was fine. Clean and in control. He didn't have the physical strength to hold the power during sex, yet that's what he craved. It was unlikely that someone bigger or stronger than him would let him be in charge, tell them what he wanted them to do, how he wanted things done to him. Until E found a way to get what he needed from sex, he'd be doing it alone. Experimenting with toys felt like an especially good idea right now. Already, he was making a shopping list in his head.

Returning to his fantasy, E stood naked in the locker room. Brian was now kissing his cheek, then gently grazing his earlobe with his teeth.

"Fuck me, Brian," E whispered, his hands gripping the man's strong biceps.

A visible shiver raked Brian's body at the words before he nodded, sending a lock of his hair to bounce on his forehead.

"Follow me." E laid down on the bench and lifted his legs.

Brian's beautiful face lit up as he stepped closer. He took a hold of E's hips and pulled him to the very edge. Brian stroked his cock, before positioning himself above E, kissing E's chest, sucking E's nipple, then releasing it with a smack of his lips. E arched at the tease, just in time to let Brian in. His cock slid inside with ease, probably lubed when E hadn't paid attention. Yes, that was easy to accomplish in a fantasy.

E reached to the base of the toy and clicked the button there. The gentle vibrations travelled through his gut, the flat tip massaging his prostate, setting E's nerve endings alight. Within moments, his entire body was heated as he undulated his hips, boner flapping on his stomach.

Holy shit, it was intense.

E released a high, mewling sound and squeezed his cock to keep himself from coming too soon.

Deep breath. And another.

Then he clicked the base of the toy again, and the vibrations intensified.

Closing his eyes, he returned to that locker room. *He was in Brian's arms, the man drilling into him, filling him just right, his hands clutching E's hips in a possessive grip.*

Brian groaned, then whispered: "You feel so good, I could fuck you all night."

E had heard Brian's voice in the uni corridor and at the SU bar often enough for him to clearly imagine it now: all low and velvety-smooth.

E sped the movements of his hand on his cock as the fantasy played in his mind, the vibrator wreaking havoc on his insides, his hand working fast, imagining it was Brian, his strong hands, his muscled body right in front of him.

Almost there.

"Will you fuck me, next?" the imaginary Brian asked.

E shot off the bed as his climax took full possession of his body. He must have looked like he was being exorcised, writhing on the bed, spurting all over himself, the duvet, and fuck knew where else. With trembling hands, he turned the vibrator off and pulled it out on a groan, his over-sensitised flesh begging for mercy. A drop of his come landed on his lip and he licked it, imagining Brian would want to taste it too, would capture it with his tongue and moan.

It was an exquisite fantasy.

Sadly, E's reality would never come close. Some-day, he would find a way to have sex on his terms and the way he wanted. But it wouldn't be with Brian or anyone like him.

Despite his wobbly legs, he managed to clean up and change the sheets before climbing back into bed. After putting his contact lenses back into the box on his bedside table, he slid his glasses up his nose. It wasn't late so he put his headphones on and played *Another Side of the Moon* on a loop before he picked up the new Stephen King paperback he'd started the day before. Just as he was settling in, he looked into the wardrobe's mirror. A skinny nerd looked back at him. E sighed, knowing he'd have to work hard to shape his life the way he wanted it to look.

The old wardrobe must have been a remnant of the previous tenants, or whoever lived here before the current owner bought it. It, as well as the wall-paper and doors, looked like it had witnessed coal miners' strikes in the eighties. Turning surroundings into motivation, E hoped that once he graduated, he could get a place with modern decor and mini-malistic style. No damask wallpaper in sight.

The next Monday was just another day on campus. E huddled in his hoodie on his way to class as the drizzle soaked the fabric covering his head. The rectangular building whose sleek, red brick looked darker than usual in the rain was a welcome sight. The entrance to the Arthur Lewis Building consisted of a set of glass panels as tall as the structure itself, and it was towards these panels that E found himself sprinting with increasing speed.

His wet trainers squeaked as he pulled his rucksack higher on his shoulder and made his way through the ultra-modern white interior that smelled of the citrus floor cleaner. The lecture was on the fourth floor, so he jogged up the stairs, nearly bumping into someone when he reached the landing.

It was just his luck that when he lifted his head, none other than Brian Withshaw was standing in front of him, in a wet t-shirt that clung to him tighter than latex, accentuating every ridge of his abdomen. Despite their lack of height difference, Brian seemed larger than life at such a close distance. E avoided looking people in the eyes, so by default, he immediately looked down to the man's lips. *Stay chill, don't do anything stupid.*

"Hi," he said, pulling his rucksack up on his shoulder. He aimed to sound casual, but he could feel heat rushing to his cheeks.

Brian's offensively perfect lips parted as if he was about to say something.

E's heart started to pound in his chest.

Brian's tongue darted over his bottom lip, making it glisten like a shiny forbidden fruit.

Well?

Just then, a tall, blond girl materialised next to Brian and hooked her arm through his. "Hey, handsome, been looking for you." She simpered, her strong Mancunian accent grating on E's nerves. As did the way she leaned forward and planted a gratuitous kiss on Brian's cheek.

"I missed you on Friday." Brian leaned into her so close his hair touched her nape. They continued walking as if E didn't exist.

E stood in place for a second longer, feeling all of his insides shrink and die inside his body. He had never felt so invisible in his life.

Get over yourself, Ernesto Grant. Stop being an idiot.

Shaking his head to clear it, E walked towards the lecture hall, massaging his sternum with the heel of his palm.

It was fine having fantasies, but he'd better keep them far from real life. At that moment, he vowed he'd never make a fool of himself like that ever again. He had years left at uni and he would make sure to find a way to have sex—lots of it—and only with people who asked him for it.

Just before stepping into the hall, E's pocket vibrated and he fished out his phone to check who it was. He frowned at the caller ID. His parents usually called on weekends, knowing he was busy with uni otherwise. Dread crept up his neck and he swiped the green icon on the screen.

"Hi Dad, you alright?"

A beat of silence.

The fact that the answer was not an immediate 'yes' sent cold sweat down E's spine.

"Dad, did something happen?"

"Hi. No, nothing happened." Dad's voice was serious, defying his words. "You got a moment?"

"Yeah, sure." E glanced at the door to the lecture hall closing behind the last students getting in, then turned around to stand in a quiet alcove in the corridor.

"Now, it's just so you're in the loop, but don't worry."

"You're scaring me. Spit it out." E was not in the habit of being rude to his parents, but the conversation was getting the best of him.

"They found something in my test results." Dad swallowed audibly.

Oh shit.

This time it was E's turn to fall silent. "What—what did they find?" He leaned back on the wall behind him for support, his wet hoodie clinging to his t-shirt underneath.

"My liver... A small surgery and some chemo and I'll be good as new. There's no plan set yet, but the doctors are hopeful." Dad's voice shook despite his clear attempt at sounding casual.

"You have cancer?" The last word barely left E's throat as it constricted. E muttered a string of curses under his breath, feeling blood drain from his face.

"Yes."

"How—" E's voice broke, his brain unable to process what his ears absorbed. "How are you feeling?"

"Normal. If I didn't have the routine check and complained about the pain in my upper abdomen, they wouldn't have found it. Bloody hell, no, I phrased it wrong. Your mother is shaking her head at me."

"I'm coming down to London." E was already leaving the campus, his wobbly legs carrying him towards his flat on autopilot.

"You don't have to. You'd miss your exams."

"No offence, but fuck the exams." E tried not to swear in front of his parents, but desperate times called for desperate measures.

"None taken." Dad chuckled but there was tiredness in his tone.

"I have nearly all my essays done for the next term, anyway. I'll be in London first thing tomorrow morning."

Unable to utter another word, E hung up and shoved the phone into his pocket.

The pouring rain had intensified, soaking E's clothes and chilling him to the bone. The cold, dark sky above mirrored the emotions swirling in E's head.

Chapter Four

Brian

The first day of the trials went bloody fantastic, to the point where several scouts approached Brian for a quick chat. No promises yet, but they seemed dazzled by his performance, which was definitely a good sign.

Tired, but determined to impress the fuck out of everyone the next day, Brian fell asleep that evening the moment his head hit the pillow.

He dreamt of shaking the hand of the guy who'd approached him earlier in the day, but this time to sign a deal to play for Manchester United. Soon after, he'd run on the field with the best players in the world. The cheering of the crowd would meet his ears as his team entered the stadium. He'd learn so much, he'd work hard to become great, making his childhood dreams come true. He'd be successful, popular, and fit, making sure his family, while never lacking anything, would be financially set for the future. Once at the top, he'd find the perfect partner who'd support his passion, talk football with him, and love to spend time together. He'd never have to work a boring job.

Well-rested, Brian woke up before the alarm and sprang off the bed, ready for day two of the trials. Humming under his breath, he brushed his teeth and padded around the house quietly so as not to wake up his flatmates. Just as he was pulling his socks out of the drawer, he winced at the sharp pain in his ankle. It was gone a moment later as he rolled it, but the ghost of pressure remained. He hoped it was just his mind playing tricks on him from stress, that today of all days, his old injury had the cheek to bother him. Plopping his arse on the bed with a grunt of frustration, he wrapped the ankle with an elastic bandage, making sure it was invisible under the sock. That way, no one would even consider that he could be not in top shape. Which he absolutely was. He'd already fucked up the trials once because of that stupid ankle injury. He wouldn't allow it to ruin his chances at stardom again.

Once in the locker room, surrounded by players visibly vibrating with excitement, Brian sat on the bench and took deep, calming breaths. It would be a great trial day, he was sure of it. He tightened his boots and stood up, ready. His football getup felt like armour before a battle and he was determined to fight well. For his future.

After the stretching and short pep talk, all players were given blue and green shirts to put on top of their own to make two teams. The game started off rough but Brian got the ball quick and ran through the defence. Excitement and determination fuelled his every movement, his muscles well-warmed-up and ready. With the wind at his back, his sole focus was to showcase his abilities while at the same time remaining a team player. It wasn't easy but he was giving his all.

The way his boots grabbed the ground with less-than-perfect stability, Brian knew it had been raining the previous night. He'd played in much worse conditions, sometimes in the pouring rain, so he knew how to move accordingly.

Seeing his teammate open on the right, he passed the ball and within moments it was back at his feet. Running like the wind, he aimed for the goal. The sound of his boot connecting with the inflated leather made everyone slow down to look. Brian joined them, watching with bated breath as the ball soared through the air as if in slow motion, escaping the gloves of the keeper by mere inches as it landed snuggly in the upper right corner.

A roar erupted, followed by pats on the back all around. It was 1:0, an incredible start.

For the next several minutes, he was blocked enough for his team to be unable to pass him the ball, but after finding an out, it was at his boot again.

His legs ate the distance, and just when he was about to pass, a defender slid on the grass to block the move. He avoided the guy, frantically looking for someone else to be open. Nope. He had to take the shot. Willing his body to push as hard as he could, he ran.

His outstretched left leg slid far on the grass. Too far.

Snap.

Fire exploded in Brian's knee as something went horribly wrong inside.

For a second, he didn't register what was happening but as the pain turned into tiny, fiery needles assaulting his knee, his right leg folded under him and he fell to the grass. Sitting on his arse, with scouts' eyes on him, he clutched his upper thigh.

No, no. It can't be. Not now. Not again.

A roar invaded Brian's head, a loud scream of denial lost in the chaos of panic.

Someone called for a medic but Brian was only hearing it through an underwater haze. The guy kneeling in front of him became blurry, as did the grass around him. Was he crying? *Bloody hell. No.*

"I'm fine. I just—"

He tried to stand up, but as his leg wasn't stable, he wobbled, and plopped back on his arse.

This wasn't happening.

Hands appeared under his armpits on both sides. Someone was helping him up. Mindless, he leaned on his human crutches and jumped on one foot off the field.

The rest happened in a daze.

The calm voice of a medic barely registered as the man touched his leg until Brian winced. Then they escorted him to the hospital to push him around on a wheelchair along bright corridors that spoke of dark times ahead.

An MRI that revealed all four ligaments had torn. A rehabilitation plan was formed. Arthroscopic surgery scheduled. Then more rehabilitation. Predicted months on crutches before he could walk. Then run. Maybe train again. Maybe not.

The doctor's calm voice barely registered, as Brian listened to instructions that included a lot of restrictions, a workout plan for his leg, and how often to take the 500mg Naproxen tablets that were supposed to ease the pain and make the swelling go away. Then he could go to uni on crutches, waiting for the surgery.

For now, he'd stay at home recovering, with a gel icepack as his best friend.

He was glad he hadn't told his family that he'd planned to take part in the trials. His parents, brother, and sister would surely have come to cheer him on, only to watch him fail. Again.

Instead, his parents were on a month-long trip to the Caribbean, his brother probably threw a party in their absence, and his sister would help him clean up the place after. Not wanting to ruin the break they all deserved, Brian texted his parents that everything was fine and he was looking forward to the upcoming end of the term.

Meanwhile, nothing was fine.

Two of his teammates got drafted; the rest continued playing on Fridays without him.

Two weeks passed with Brian sleeping and refusing to get out of bed except to wobble to the loo. Alice visited from time to time, running her gentle fingers through his hair. Instead of soothing, the touch was annoying, only reminding him that he didn't feel like fooling around with her. At one point, he reminded her that he wouldn't mind if she hooked up with someone else. After all, their relationship had never been exclusive in theory, but seeing relief in Alice's shoulders at his words was quite a slap on the face, nonetheless. It was still shit to become a faulty piece of equipment because he couldn't be in the mood to fuck.

His flatmates brought him magazines and takeout, staying a moment longer to tell him about their day.

Brian was grateful to all of them, he truly was, but he was too furious at the world to show it, remaining resentful of the chatter about him getting better. His friends encouraged him with stories of professional footballers who, after suffering similar injuries, returned to playing eventually. Brian knew those stories from magazines. Those players had never returned to their former glory, either physically or career-wise. Their fame had died down, even if their body had healed.

It was possible that Brian's knee, after surgery and rehabilitation, would work well, but he was sure that neither his physical form nor his headspace would ever be the same. No one understood what he was going through and he was too tired to explain. He'd always been a dreamer, but it was time to stop being so naïve.

Days came and went even though his leg felt better, the bleak vision of his future was like a boulder on his shoulders, pulling him down, making dark thoughts swirl in his head.

He knew what it was.

He'd struggled with bouts of depression since his teenage years, so hiding the darkness in his head was a skill he'd mastered quite early, by having a smile on his face, neat clothes, and vibrant social life. Since he'd never been suicidal, all his doctors told him to take his time and stay positive, encouraging him that he was doing exceptionally well.

If they'd only known.

With clarity way too intense for his comfort, Brian could still remember the days following his ankle injury three years ago.

His parents took him home to recuperate, to rest in the comfort of his own room. Surrounded by posters of successful players, stacks of football magazines, memorabilia and awards, he felt like every single item had been mocking him, telling him that he wasn't good enough and never would be.

After a week, his parents had to return to work, and his siblings continued to go to school as normal, leaving Brian alone in the house, with plenty of food, snacks, and video games. He had no interest in any of those.

Instead, he crept to his parents' room. With his ankle nearly back to normal, he felt like a fraud, but he had plans and was determined to realise them. He'd been waiting for a perfect moment for days, ready to use the opportunity once it arose. When he opened his Dad's side of the wardrobe, the dark hum in his head intensified and he wanted to feed it. His heart pounded in his chest so fast, he could feel the rush in his face and in his ears. Something bigger than him was directing his movements. He watched his hand reach towards his Dad's belts on a hanger, feeling their textures, tracing them with his fingertips. Pulling one with a distinct creak, he inspected it closely. It was perfect for the job. The metal buckle clanked as he pulled the end of the belt through it before putting it around his neck. The smell of worn leather was intense in his nose, and his shoulders relaxed as a sense of calm washed over him. It was nearly over.

He would be free.

Free of expectations and responsibilities, free of dreams he'd never be able to fulfil.

On his way towards the door and the handle he knew was sturdy enough for the job, he stopped at the full-length mirror on the wall.

When he met his own reflection, his content smile disappeared, and he let his arms fall to the sides. A slim boy of 18 looked back at him. A boy with bags under his eyes from lack of sleep, pale skin from the lack of sun, with clothes hanging off him from not eating or exercising for the last week. That boy had a family who loved him, who cared about him, and had to see him in this state. Broken.

They didn't deserve that.

Brian's mind recalled his Mum's face, smiling when she picked him up from primary school, his Dad laughing when they kicked the ball in their small rear garden. He saw his younger brother, Brendan, who cheered him from the stands during every Sunday football league game when they were children. He recalled his sister, Beatrice, who was always there for him, tutoring him for his school-

work, listening intently when he needed to rant about everything and nothing.

All of them deserved better.

And so did the boy in the mirror. Nearly a man, with a future ahead of him. Maybe a bright one, maybe not. But one with people around him who supported him fully.

Right then, the belt around his neck ceased to be a line to freedom and became a noose about to cut his life short. It was heavy and hot, nearly burning his flesh.

It didn't belong there.

Brian's legs buckled and he folded himself to plop on the floor taking short, shallow breaths as if he was unable to take in enough air into his lungs to survive.

With trembling hands, he ripped the belt off his neck and tossed it aside. Chest heaving, he crab-walked away from the evil leather cobra: poised and ready to strike with gleaming chrome teeth, daring him to commit the deed he knew could never be undone.

Hurtling back to the present, Brian looked in the direction of his wardrobe, full of clothes, football gear, and belts... This time, none of them called to him. *Thank fuck.* He exhaled in relief, sagging back into the pillows. The movement brought up the scent of the sheets and as he caught a whiff, he grimaced.

Bloody hell, he stank like the fridge in the flat after they'd lost power for two days last month. Or rather, he and his bed stank like a man who needed to take steps to get his damn life in order. Small steps would suffice. Like taking a shower.

Chapter Five

Brian

Horrified by his own stench, Brian sat up in bed. For the three weeks since he sprained his knee, he'd rested more than necessary, so the swelling had completely come down and his leg looked normal. Sort of. Both his legs were less toned after near disuse for weeks, a far cry from the toned look he'd been working on so hard for most of his life. He had two months left until the scheduled procedure to rebuild his ligaments but he'd been ignoring phone calls from the rehabilitation centre where he was supposed to work on his muscles to help with post-surgery recovery.

Brian rolled his legs off the bed and wiggled his toes, watching the last rays of the sun that streamed through the parted drapes play on his skin.

Standing up, he gently put weight on his right leg. He didn't even wince as it wobbled and the unpleasant sensation of tiny needles prickled inside. With a grunt of frustration, he plopped back down and reached for his phone on the bedside table. Invitations for a party blew up the screen when he turned it on. It was probably why the house was so quiet, everyone had already left.

Brian weighed his options. By no means did he feel any better, but he was sick of staying in the room. Technically, he could go to the party on crutches. Since the accident, he'd been using one crutch to go to the loo, but both if he moved around the house. He just wouldn't drink because of the meds he was still taking. He didn't need alcohol to have a good time, anyway. Or at least, a better time than he was having alone in a place that smelled like a locker room after an intense game in July.

Getting into the tub was a test of skill and agility, but he managed to shower without further damage to his leg. Brian could sense his mood elevate as the foul body odour he'd cultivated washed away down the drain. He felt lighter; as if the soap and water cleansed not only his body, but also his mind.

He patted himself dry and left the towel in the bathroom. Thanks to the house being empty, he didn't have to cover his nudity to limp to his room on crutches.

The old hinges on the curtain rails squeaked as Brian pulled them apart, letting the warm glow of twilight flood the room. When he opened the window, the pleasant July evening chill whooshed over his face and bare chest, along with the noise of students celebrating their Friday freedom. Most of them were probably already done with exams for the year, while Brian would have to take his at a later date, if the professors proved to be understanding of his injury. They might not. After all, he hadn't hurt his head; his entire body was well enough for him to attend the exams. Yet his mind was far from fine.

He didn't have the energy to deal with stupid exams just yet.

Putting the issue aside, he slid open the wardrobe doors, revealing a mess of clean clothes, thrown in haphazardly after he'd done the washing the last time. The hangers were full of football shirts, a stack of football shorts sat to the side, and on the floor lay his duffel bag and running shoes.

Bile rose to his throat at the sight of every item that reminded him of his failure. Swallowing hard, he reached to the very bottom of the stack of clothes to pull out his old comfort shirt—a faded black tee with a Guns N' Roses logo on it. After adding some worn-out jeans with ripped knees and plain trainers, his outfit was complete except for one thing: an ugly hinged knee brace. Brian didn't want to wear it, but he knew it was necessary. Raking a hand through the damp hair that reached his nape, he declared himself ready to leave.

Brian paused with his hand on the doorknob and turned around to look at the dishevelled bed he'd been sweating into for way too long. With a few quick tugs, he tossed the bedding to the floor, making sure he'd have to change the sheets when he returned. Depending on how the evening would go, there was a risk of him ending up back in bed and unwilling to leave it for a while again.

Wallet, phone, keys.

Sigh. My house key is still in the sodding duffel.

Brian returned to the wardrobe, trying not to pay attention to the contents of his bag as he extracted the key from the side pocket.

Thankfully, the flat was only on the first floor. So, after some manoeuvring and figuring out how to use his crutches on the stairs, he was finally out of the building. The scent of freshly-cut grass mixed with air saturated with alcohol and cigarette smoke hit Brian's nose as students passed him by. He didn't even have to look at his messages to know where the party his mates had gone to was; at George's posh estate, or rather—his parents'. Brian had been to that place so many times by now he could wobble there blindfolded.

Yet, he wasn't moving.

Leaning forward, putting his weight on the crutches, he realised he had no intention of going to George's house. He didn't want to see his teammates. Or Alice. Or anyone else from his crowd.

The dull emptiness inside him was like a concrete room—everything echoed off the walls, but no sound could be heard on the outside. He embodied that room, and for now, wasn't ready to let any sound in or out of it. Wasn't ready to tell anyone how he felt, or let anyone back into his life.

Aimlessly, with his crutches clicking against the pavement, he wandered towards a bus stop.

Sod this.

He should get on a bus to the station. Then take a random train and just go somewhere far. Far from Manchester, from school, his flat, his friends. Far from everything that reminded him of his failure.

The hot-aired *tsss* of the bus stopping right in front of him made him look up. A group of excited students poured out of it like fans after a successful ball game. Except their bags were full of clinking glass bottles and their party attire was a mish-mash of jeans, hoodies, piercings, tattoos, and combat boots. *Yeah, no.* They looked completely different to football fans and were definitely not Brian's usual crowd.

"Hey, are you going to the party at Micah's?" A girl with short, bright-pink hair eyed Brian up and down, taking in his overgrown locks and scruffy black t-shirt.

Taken aback, Brian hesitated, then nodded. *Maybe this is what I need—a change of crowd and scenery.* "Yeah, can I tag along?"

The group slowed their pace to match Brian's, but none of them asked what happened to him. Maybe they didn't care, or maybe they were just respecting his privacy. Either way, Brian was glad he didn't have to discuss it.

Soon enough, they entered a dingy block of flats. At the sight of it, Brian dreaded climbing the stairs, but thankfully, it had a lift. After enduring a sardine-can journey to the third floor, Brian followed the group towards blaring music coming from one of the flats.

The smell of weed, beer, and sweat hit Brian's nose as they entered, and the familiar mix set him on edge. He'd always been the life of the party, finding a way to talk to everyone; have a laugh with any new additions to their group. This, however, was not his crowd. There were a handful of people he vaguely recognised from the campus but no one he actually knew.

The noises surrounding him were not of football on the telly, clinking beer bottles, and wolf whistles at the ladies—things he was used to hearing at George's place. The entire party was the antithesis of the ones he'd attended since he started uni.

Fighting the urge to bolt, Brian took a seat on a chair in the corner of the main living area where the floor was littered with cushions and a big sofa sat in the centre. The oldies R&B and rock music floating in the air put him at ease, filling his bones with melodies of comfort. He recognised *Tracks of my Tears* by Smokey Robinson & The Miracles and thought the lyrics quite apt to what he was feeling. Genuine laughter and gasps to the side made him turn his head to see a group of people sitting cross-legged on the carpet playing what looked like a weird-as-fuck board game with way too many dice.

"Hey, you want a drink?" A bloke with long black hair nudged Brian on the shoulder.

"I'm good, thanks." Brian hadn't brought anything, so he didn't feel entitled to freebies.

"You sure? We got beer, cider, vodka..." Long-hair bit his lip, looking at Brian, then the crutches he'd leaned against the wall. The sight of the man's teeth grazing his lip brought heat to Brian's cheeks and he let his gaze fall to the loose shirt but very tight jeans he wore. "How about juice or Coke?"

Suddenly hot and thirsty as hell, Brian nodded. "Coke sounds great, thanks."

"Fab. I'll get you one."

Moments later, Brian let the cold, fizzy drink soothe the heat in his body as it travelled down his throat. He'd taken his pain meds that morning, but despite them waning, he didn't want to add alcohol into the mix. Missing the evening dose, however, meant his knee pulsed with pressure-pain.

Somehow, he blended in to the point no one seemed to question his presence at the party. Then again, as he looked around, he realised no one matched and yet, for that exact reason, everyone did. The somewhat bohemian group was still talking energetically over the board game, while next to them several people with clothing all colours of the rainbow and glitter in their hair stood chatting next to two goth girls dressed in black with arms around each other.

In the other corner, a bloke with huge-arse glasses sat next to a laptop connected to the sound system, switching between metal, punk, and classic rock. The next tune was *Have You Ever* by The Offspring, resonating with quick melody and strong lyrics. A moment later, a gorgeous woman with thick thighs and breasts falling out of her corset sat on the bespectacled dude's lap and kissed the daylights out of him. That seemed to have switched the mood as Brian noticed more couples getting amorous, from the two goth girls kissing to three blokes groping and necking on the sofa. One of them was Long-hair. He was sitting on the lap of a large guy—probably in his early thirties—with short-cropped hair and a neat, red beard. *Dayum, all that muscle.* Redbeard must be either a rugby player or a bodybuilder. Long-hair was grinding his hips in a dance-like rhythm while the third guy, around Brian's age with a fringe covering half his face, was kissing Long-hair's neck before joining their lips.

Brian sat mesmerised, feeling lava flow through his veins down to his cock. He looked down as if needing to double-check if his reaction was real, only to see a clear bulge in his jeans.

Brian straightened in his seat, recalling his doubts from before the injury. He'd always been certain that every man could admire another man's shape, defined muscles, or strong jaw. It wasn't unusual to notice their full lips, thick lashes, or nice smile. He'd never had the courage to ask, but the several times he'd commented on his mate's physical features when in the locker room, he'd gotten strange looks in return, or an odd homophobic joke thrown his way. He'd laugh it up, shrug and move on, but there was always a sense of shame tingling at his nape. Watching the men in front of him be so openly sexual in their attraction to each other made Brian lean in towards his earlier suspicions.

He might not be 100% straight after all.

It didn't matter, though, as he shouldn't indulge in his curiosity, because—

He frowned, his train of thought skidding to a halt and flopping on its arse like a ball player on wet grass.

I can do whatever the fuck I want with my body. And maybe then, I won't have to wonder.

His football career was surely over. And if he had no chance of going pro, he could experiment. He had nothing to lose. If he was anything other than straight, it wouldn't be that big of a deal anymore, right? The people at this party didn't look shamed, or shy about it. It was awe-inspiring. Even the commotion coming from the kitchen couldn't distract Brian until someone ran in to grab Long-hair, telling him something about food burning in the oven. The man's absence left Redbeard's thick thighs exposed, making the hard-on imprint in his jeans difficult to miss.

He must have been staring too hard as Redbeard's gaze locked on his. The big dude crooked a finger and Brian looked around, making sure the gesture was meant for him.

The guy laughed, a low, rumbling sound that travelled like music through the air.

With as much grace as he could muster, Brian pushed himself up and reached for his crutches.

"Care to sit on Daddy's lap?" came the melodic rumble.

"I'm sorry, what?" Brian snapped his head up as confusion flooded his brain. He was now a mere two feet away from the guy, watching him chuckle.

"'Scuse me for being forward. I'm Arran," the big man said, his Scottish accent as thick as honey. "And this is Rod."

"Hi." The younger guy next to Arran offered a chin nod.

"Brian." He reached out to fist-bump Arran and Rod on the other side of the big man.

"Ye need help?" Arran reached out for Brian but didn't touch him.

"I'm good, thanks." Brian took the two steps to the sofa and dropped next to Arran. Maybe he was forward but he made it clear he was interested in Brian without an ounce of hesitation. How extraordinary. Brian paused, his thigh flush with Arran's. He'd never been so close to a man who he could openly appreciate without making it weird. Brian took in Arran's wide chest with shirt open just enough to show a dusting of hair, and the man's arms that could probably bench Brian's weight. He fully expected his fight-or-flight response to kick in at the sight. He should be ashamed or at least hesitant.

Yet what he found inside himself were none of those. His heart beat faster, overwhelmed by curiosity and a need that he'd been hiding way too long. His blood couldn't decide if it wanted to fill his cheeks or his cock. He wanted Arran to touch him. What was more, he wanted Rod's attention too. He turned his gaze to the younger guy on the other side. Rod was staring at Redbeard in awe—as if he not only wanted him, but wanted to *be* him. Then Rod's eyes met Brian's and lit up like a football field during a night game. *It couldn't be that easy.*

"Dinnae be shy." Arran smiled in a way that Lucifer must have smiled both as an angel and after his fall. If only Lucifer was Scottish. His open shirt showing off his rugby-player physique made Brian realise that all that skin was on offer. To touch? To lick? He wasn't sure, but he had a feeling that if he didn't find out now, he would regret it.

"I'm not. I'm just..." He swallowed, sitting up sideways to see the men better. "Looking." What was he saying? He wasn't browsing shelves.

"I'll be straight with ye, Brian." Arran rolled his eyes at the snicker coming from Rod at the words. "Rod here is, how tae say it, my protégé, and I'm teaching him how tae satisfy men, if ye ken ma meaning."

Brian opened his mouth to say that he wasn't experienced but Aaron shut him up with one raised finger.

"Lemme finish. All I'm offering is a night you'd definitely remember. Ye wouldna ha tae do much, promise. I see ye ha some situation goin' on with yer leg."

"Knee."

"Yer knee. So we'd mack sure ye'd be comfortable." Arran sat back, draping his massive arms over the sofa's backrest. "Just think about it."

Brian's first reaction was to refuse but as seconds passed without his reply, Arran reached out for his hair. Brian didn't flinch but let the man tuck a loose strand behind his ear before resting his palm on Brian's cheek.

Parting his lips, Brian's breathing quickened as he nodded. He wasn't sure what exactly he was agreeing to, but he was sure he wanted to find out.

Arran leaned in slowly, as if trying not to spook Brian. Brian could turn his head away with ease, he could say no.

Instead, he let the warm lips of another man claim his own for the first time.

It was just a peck, but when Arran was pulling away, Brian snapped his hand around the guy's neck to pull him back. This time, the kiss was deep and he let experience in that department guide him. The biggest difference was Arran's beard scratching his face, a sensation he'd never experienced before. The kiss, however, felt like something he was supposed to do, like he'd learned a new skill on the field and was ready to reach for more. It wasn't a football field, but it was one he was willing to play on tonight.

"Not shy, after all." Arran smiled crookedly as he slowly pulled away. His eyes filled with lust as he adjusted his hard-on. He leaned in again, but this time, his lips grazed Brian's cheek. "Ye can lay on the bed with yer legs up and let Rod eat yer bonny arse," he said in a low rumble that sent shivers down Brian's spine as he pictured the scenario. "Then he'll suck yer cock and finger yer hole 'till you come. I hope you'd ask real nice to come wi' ma cock in yer mouth until I'd be ready to paint yer chest white.

Mebbe ask Rod tae join me. How does that sound, eh?"

"It sounds—" Brian cleared his throat, his cock swelling, his mind reeling. "It sounds great."

"Fan-fucking-tastic!" Rod slapped his hands on his thighs as he stood up. If eating Brian's arse made him that enthusiastic, who was Brian to say no?

"You sure?" Arran asked, remaining seated.

But Brian was already reaching for Rod's out-stretched hand. "Yeah."

The two men helped him get up and escorted him to a tiny bedroom. If he didn't enjoy this night with two hot blokes ready to show him a good time, he would definitely know that he was straight. If he enjoyed it, it would probably bring more questions than answers, but he would worry about that later.

He could have remained in bed alone, or taken more of those lovely pain meds they'd prescribed. Alternatively, he could have drowned his sorrow in alcohol and drunk himself into a stupor. He was only too aware that banishing the darkness which lurked inside his head was a formidable task. How-ever, he was determined to succeed even if he'd have to turn his life upside down trying. He needed to get lost in pleasure, to have someone guide him and make him forget how his life was about to be different from what he'd dreamed of.

Maybe fucking his brains out was the best solu-tion of them all.

It was time to find out.

Chapter Six

Ernesto

E woke up with a grunt at the sharp pain in his side, before realising it had been caused by Latif's elbow. His brother has always been subtle like that. Straightening up in his chair, E tilted his head until his neck cracked. He looked around the waiting room, realising he'd fallen asleep waiting for his dad in the hospital.

"Is he out? Do we know anything?" E blinked a few times, clearing his vision to see Mum's long, black hair falling to her mid-back.

"Here he is!" Mum shot out of her chair, her slender frame full of energy as she bolted down the corridor towards Dad.

Latif followed her and E did the same, joining the family jog through the oncology wing.

"Perfectly clear." Dad grinned, spreading his arms, presenting his thinned-out but cancer-free body.

"Oh, thank fuck." Mum exhaled a breath of relief, visibly reeling to the point she nearly wobbled on her feet.

Latif reached out to steady her, but she grabbed his wrist and pulled him close, then did the same to E as she wrapped her arms around Dad.

The past several months had been a strain on the family, with everyone worrying about Dad's liver cancer. After surgery and weeks of chemo, it seemed they could now breathe easy. Dad had tried to stay positive throughout the process, but the days when he'd been too weak to get up had been especially horrible. It must have been a nightmare for him, and seeing him suffer had been hard on E and the entire family. E had decided to spend the summer holidays in London at Mum's side, driving her and Dad to every appointment in between the part-time data-entry job he'd taken for the few weeks off uni. He had always seen Dad as the strongest and most reliable man on the planet, and with his resilience and sense of humour in the face of adversity, the man had proved that it was the ultimate truth. E hoped that Dad would never have to go through anything like that again.

"What did they say?" Latif steered Dad and Mum towards the exit and to their car.

"They'll have to test me every now and then." Dad shrugged, reaching for Mum's hand. "Apparently, these things tend to come back even if I'm completely clear now."

E followed them in a daze, slowly processing the information his Dad was detailing. The fear of losing a parent had put his life into perspective and made him analyse his approach to it.

He'd decided to finish his studies in Manchester, taking advantage of the campus to focus on learning and his new gym routine. But beyond that, he needed to get out there and face his fears. He was determined to find a way to do it that worked with his neurodiversity.

As they all squished into Dad's car, with Latif driving and E in the back with Mum, E looked through the window, still registering every word his family said. Dad asked about Latif's girlfriend and the news of them moving in together. Serena was a nice girl and in tune with Latif's open outlook on life, gender, and sexuality, earning their parents' approval fairly quickly.

"Ernie, did you tell Mum that you signed up for Spanish society at uni?" Latif looked at E in the rearview mirror, bringing him into the conversation.

"Have you really?" Mum turned to him with the kind of radiant smile that he'd seen so rarely in the past weeks.

"Yeah. I want to know it better." E nodded, tapping a rhythm on his thigh with his fingers. "For myself. And I'd like to surprise Abuela when we go to visit her next time."

"She'll love that," Mum cooed, reaching to squeeze E's hand.

Despite Mum being a native speaker, the phrases E knew best were mostly the curse words she mumbled under her breath occasionally and the endearments she used towards her sons and husband. Other than that, Mum and Dad spoke English at home. Since he'd refused to learn Spanish as a child, they didn't want to push him, especially as he hadn't started communicating verbally until after he'd turned four. Now, he felt the need to know his mother's native language better. Due to his neurodivergence, he didn't like aeroplanes—the noise, the crowds, and, most importantly, the smells. So his parents hadn't taken him to Spain very often. His lack of exposure to the language led to him knowing it very little. He vowed to himself that would change as one of the first steps of his long-term self-care plan.

"What are you grinning about?" E turned to his flatmate, who sauntered into the sitting room as if he had the best news to share.

"I was invited to this party that I wanted to go to for months. Finally!" Rod punched the air.

"Oh?" E straightened in his seat on the sofa, eager to hear what had caused such a spring in his friend's step.

"Sorry, it's by invitation only, so I can't take anyone with me. Besides, I don't think you'd like it there." Rod plopped on the sofa, sinking into the worn cushions.

"Why wouldn't I?" E frowned, not sure if he managed to hide his disappointment. It was one thing not to be invited to the popular students' parties, and completely different not to be invited by his friend.

"It's just..." Rod shrugged, then leaned back on the sofa, looking at the ceiling. "It's sexual in theme."

"So?"

"You rarely have sex with people."

"You know jack shit, Rod." E stood up to pace the floor.

"Don't shoot me!" Rod raised his hands in surrender.

"Whatever, just go party with your new boyfriend."

"For the thousandth time, Arran is not my boyfriend. It's more complicated than that."

E rolled his eyes. "Sure it is. Since you met him, you don't want to talk about where you're off to, or even who he is. It's not like you, just saying."

"Okay, I'm sorry. I'm a shit friend. It's a bit hard to explain. So I'll work my way to it." He patted the seat next to him on the sofa and E took it, facing his friend. "But first, will you tell me what is it that you're looking for in sex?"

"Control," E replied without having to think it through.

"What?" Rod bristled, so taken aback his eyebrows disappeared into his fringe. "How so?"

"I want to touch and be touched only on my terms and the way I want." It felt good to finally say what he secretly wanted. "But that's never gonna happen. Every time I meet a guy at a bar or someone sets me up on a date, they get all handsy with their sticky fingers and lolling tongue."

Rod snorted, shaking his head.

"It's not funny. Do you know how annoying that is? Puts me off sex with them completely."

"No, no, that sounds quite horrible. You'd like someone willing to give you control over how the sex is going to happen?"

"Yeah." *How does he know?*

"Maybe give you their body to play with, as long as you respect their boundaries too."

"Exactly. I know it's fucked up. I just can't deal with not knowing what's going to happen and no one agrees to bedroom scenarios beforehand. I thought I was weird before, but the more I think about it, the more I realise I'm a lost cause. It will be me, my hand, and my growing box of sex toys for the rest of my life." E was aware of the dramatic tone of his voice, but he didn't care.

"Your what?"

"You don't want to know." He thought of the many trips to the local adult shop and to several more in London's Soho.

"Actually, I do. But not for the reasons you might think."

"I don't understand."

"Fuck." Rod sighed, pulling his fringe down. "We've never talked about sex at length, you just told me that you don't like some textures and hair."

"It's not personal, you know it."

"Yeah, yeah." Rod waved a hand in dismissal then took a deep breath. "Arran is sort of my mentor. He teaches me how to be a dom—I mean a dominant in bed."

"There are lessons for that?" E leaned forward, his curiosity peaked.

"Well, no. For now, he's just kind of telling me and showing me how it works before I do anything. Giving me instructions when I have sex."

"Wait, so he's there when you have sex?"

"At first, no, but a few months ago, we were at this party and an opportunity arose to umm... play with this guy and Aaron instructed me what to do to give him pleasure. It was hot as fuck." Rod whistled low before grinning at the look on E's face. "See, your ideas are not as weird as you thought."

"So, he controlled the situation, then." E wouldn't rest until he knew everything. Anything that would suggest there were people who saw sex the way he had was a goldmine to him.

"Yes, that's because I need to learn how to do it, what the possibilities are, and what I want to do to another person or have done to me. After that, yeah, I can have a scenario for the person to agree on beforehand and change it only as we discuss in the meantime if needed."

"Could you tell them not to touch you? Or when and where and how to touch you?"

"Yeah, if that's what they'll be willing to do from the start. Some people get off on that. On being told what to do during sex."

E's mind was soaking in the information like a sponge and he waved at his friend to continue.

"I can give you a list of websites for research. So you could see what BDSM is and read up on it. I got a whole sheet of them from Arran and it's been very educational. Some stuff is not for me, but the beauty of it is that you can pick and choose. The most important thing is consent. So that goes for mere touching, too."

"That sounds a lot safer and less creepy than going to a pub."

"Right? I have little practical knowledge for now, but Arran said that his friends are opening this club in London—it's not the first one there by any means, but it's something they've decided to open together. It would be BDSM-centred, with strict rules and no touching without consent."

"Sounds fantastic," E breathed.

"It does. Once you read all about it, and if you're still interested, I'll get you an invite to the next party. Maybe we could go to the club's opening in a few months, too?"

"What's it called?"

"Handcuffs something, hmm... Golden Handcuffs! Pretty neat, huh? Very on brand, I suppose."

"Handcuffs. Right." E imagined toned men entering a stage to perform strip-tease, dressed in police uniforms, dangling handcuffs and more.

"Yeah, I'm just grazing the surface of what the world has to offer, and I'm already loving it," Rod said with excitement.

That evening and the entire following week, E read through the links, watched videos, and got a subscription to a porn site. Despite little gay content, it was useful nonetheless. Next week, Rod was taking him to a house party with kink themes where people had to respect each other's boundaries. That didn't mean that it excluded the possibility of E having a good time with another man.

He didn't need or want a relationship. He had school to finish and a career to start, and wouldn't want to deal with anyone who'd try to change him. Having sex with partners willing to follow instructions? Oh yeah, that was definitely what he needed.

New mindset, firm goals, solid plan—E was determined to transform his life.

He was still miffed at Brian for being such a privileged, ignorant arsehole. Nevertheless, E had to indulge his curiosity, so got into his car and drove to the sports centre to watch the first match of the new term.

Sitting on the hood of his Beetle, notebook in hand, he couldn't help but notice that Brian was nowhere to be seen. Maybe it was for the best. E was done making a fool of himself. Now, he was ready to embrace his needs and build his life around them with detailed precision. Maybe he'd even return to wearing glasses.

THE END

I hope you enjoyed this bittersweet tale of Brian and E's early days. Never fear—they'll get their happily ever after in the end!

If you'd like to find out how this happens, Brian and E's story continues in my novel "The Blindfold

Date." The couple will appear in subsequent books in Pursuit of Love series as minor/side characters, as well as in bonus scenes for my newsletter subscribers.

If you're here because you've already read The Blindfold Date: thank you from the bottom of my heart for your support. You can check out future books coming out in Pursuit of Love series on my Amazon author profile: author.to/KCCarmine

If you enjoyed the story and would like to leave a review, you can do so on Amazon, Goodreads, Bookbub, any social media or blog. I appreciate every kind word and review. Thank you for reading!

Suicide prevention helplines:
USA: 1 800 273 TALK (8255)
UK and Ireland: 116 123 / 0800 689 5652
Australia: 13 11 14
Canada: 1 800 6686868
Germany: 0800 111 0 111

The Blindfold Date: Chapter One

The Date — Ernesto

T he cold water Ernesto splashed on his face did nothing to calm his nerves. He exited the bathroom and immediately tucked himself into the corridor alcove in 'Adonis and Pomegranate', an up-and-coming Marylebone restaurant.

He was still considering bailing on his date.

Toying nervously with the beaded bracelet his nieces had made him, he twisted its components until his heart returned to its normal rhythm.

For years, Ernesto had enjoyed casual sex made safe by the rules of the club he frequented but—upon reaching thirty-two—he'd decided it was time to look for something more permanent. His friends had set him up on dates that had ended up being several hours of awkward conversation and him trying to wriggle out of meeting again to 'give it another shot' when he already knew it would be fruitless. The worst part was bumping into some of those candidates weeks later at parties with mutual friends or, even worse, at a shop, waving awkwardly over a pack of cherry tomatoes. He knew he wasn't the nerd everyone ignored at uni anymore: he'd taken his future into his own hands, embraced who he was, and made accommodations that worked with his lifestyle and neurodiversity. Now, he hoped he was ready for a relationship. If only there was someone out there who was ready for someone like him.

After learning of The Blindfold Date app, Ernesto had decided to try it out. The rules were simple: each profile had basic information and a clothed body shot but no picture of the face. Once you matched with someone, you met at a restaurant in your area that had partnered with the app. Its immense success had led many restaurants to offer the requisite services in hopes of attracting new clientele and marketing, the upfront fee guaranteeing them income even if the date ended prematurely. You and your date were led to a table blindfolded. Each party had three questions to ask the other. If both parties liked the answers, they could take off their blindfolds and continue the date. If not, they would be escorted out by the staff, never to see each other's faces—therefore avoiding the awkward post-failed-date conversation or random meeting in the future. Ernesto matched with a man only two years his senior at thirty-five, whose body appealed to him, and whose answers about sexual preferences sounded like he was open to trying new things. It was good enough for a first try. Although if he found the date format not to his liking, he might never use it again.

For his first Blindfold Date, Ernesto had picked a restaurant close to his flat in Marylebone so he could get home quickly in case the date was a complete disaster.

Now, he tugged on his cuff to hide the bracelet and re-tucked his shirt into his light wash jeans. Looking into his reflection in the corridor mirror, he made sure his blue faux hawk hairstyle looked as presentable as he could make it. He'd considered dyeing it his natural dark brown, but he liked it the way it was, and if his date didn't, then that was their problem, not his.

"I'll escort you to your table whenever you're ready, Mr Grant," the maître d', a tall woman with a pleasant smile, told him. He wanted to tell her to call him 'E,' as most people in his life referred to him. But she was neither his friend nor family, so he swallowed the urge. The blindfold she was holding was similar to a sleep mask, fluffy and black, and the sight of it made Ernesto's stomach clench and his heart beat faster.

"I'm ready, thank you." He swallowed hard, offered her a smile, and removed his glasses so she could secure the blindfold in place. She led him to the table by his elbow, narrating what was in front of him so he wouldn't trip, until he was seated in a chair.

"Your date is ready for you, sir," the Maître d' whispered into E's ear. The wait staff knew not to use proper names, as was the protocol.

Ernesto liked to be in control of his life and decide which people were a part of it. Having few to no surprises in his daily routine was a comfort he relied on, and despite tonight being a step out of his comfort zone, it was still orchestrated enough for him to give it a shot. After all, if he didn't like the other guy when they had both answered the three questions, he could just leave.

For most of his life, he'd found it hard to read people, to understand what they were thinking or feeling. But through careful practice, he'd taught himself to recognise the correlation between what and how he said things and other people's reactions. It was easier during sexual play, as people tended to be a lot more expressive, and not only verbally. Social interaction had always been his weakest point, as was true of so many at his end of the neurodiversity scale.

"It's my first time doing this."

The smooth, low voice came from directly in front of Ernesto. The table must have been small, as the man sounded incredibly close. E slid his foot forward until he bumped into the other man's shoe to confirm it before pulling away.

"Mine, too. You can start with your first question," Ernesto said, and carefully arranged what he hoped would be a disarming smile onto his features before remembering it would be wasted on the blindfolded man in front of him. His throat felt dry but even if there was a glass of water on the table, he wouldn't want to risk reaching for it and knocking it over.

"Your profile said you're a programmer. What do you write code for? And do you like it?"

Those were *two* questions, but E was willing to let that slide. What a disappointing choice, though, asking about work.

"Video games. And yeah, I love it." Short and simple answer. Ernesto hoped the questions would get better. "Do you play video games?" he asked, smoothing his sweaty palms on his jeans, feeling the tablecloth brush his wrists.

"Only when I have someone to play with," the man replied with a flirty note to his tone.

Okay, so he was a multiplayer game guy. Not too bad. He was unlikely to be familiar with C++ or any other coding language, but there was hope yet that he wouldn't begrudge E's profession or hobbies.

"What do your friends call you?" the man asked and Ernesto could hear him shift by the rustle of fabric and creaking of his chair. He was nervous too.

"E. It's a short form of my name," Ernesto explained, not giving away his full name before he was ready to take the blindfold off. "Your profile said your perfect date would be a picnic on a grassy hill. Why?"

"I have nothing against a restaurant or a movie and takeout on the sofa, but the idea of a relaxing afternoon on a hilltop with a beautiful view sounds amazing. I would see anyone who was approaching so we wouldn't be interrupted. And at sunset," the man sighed, a smile clear in his voice, "the view would be wonderful."

E found himself speechless, imagining the described evening in detail and the sheer romance of it. Of course, his date might have prepared that answer in advance and taken a shot in the dark that E was a romantic. The privacy of such a date sounded wonderful in contrast to restaurants and other social spaces with their complicated rules of interaction. Those were the kind of things that often eluded E.

"My turn. What's the place on your body that's sensitive but neglected by lovers?" the man asked next, his voice low.

A choked sound left E as he felt his cheeks flame.

The man must have picked up on E's shock at the forward question as it made him backtrack. "I'm sorry if that's—"

"My earlobes," E interrupted, then swallowed, trying not to imagine this faceless man sensually licking his earlobes when both of them were naked in bed. How would it feel to have this stranger beneath him, his voice so peculiarly familiar, whispering into E's ear, his body writhing, his hands tied above his head...? "We're out of questions," E said breathlessly, trying to keep his libido together. He straightened in his seat to relieve the pressure his jeans put on his thickening cock.

"I'm okay to just chat if you'd like. Or—" The man hesitated as if he was just as aware as E that either of them could simply end the date now.

"It's ridiculous, but your voice reminds me of someone I used to know," E said. He closed his eyes behind the mask, allowing himself to imagine the man he used to watch play footie when they were at uni. The man whose body he could still picture with ease, even if he hadn't seen him for nearly a decade.

"Did you like him?" It was a casual question and E felt like he had nothing to lose by letting a stranger know that he fancied some guy years before.

"I had a crush on him for years, but I don't think he even knew I existed." E chuckled, feeling the old longing settling within his chest.

"I'm glad," his date replied, his tone low as if he'd swallowed a gulp of scotch and it was still burning on its way down.

"Why?"

"Maybe if he had, you wouldn't be here, on this date with me."

E snorted. This guy was a smooth talker, but there was no way to determine if his compliments were genuine, especially if E couldn't see his face. He would have to risk it and hope he was not making a huge mistake. "I'm ready to take the blindfold off, but you can ask me something else if you like before that."

"No."

E's stomach sunk, but he thrust his chin up and was ready to say goodbye before the man spoke again.

"I meant that I don't need to ask anything else. I want to see you, and I'm ready to take mine off, too."

Oh. E bit his cheek to prevent a grin from overtaking his face. By the way his date was eager to continue after such a short conversation, E surmised that the man was much more outgoing than E had ever been, braver to engage with new people. Despite an inner urge to abandon ship and stick to pre-arranged encounters in the well-controlled confines of the club, E knew this might be his chance to get out of his shell. Clearly, his date was on the same page.

E's stomach had been knotted in anticipation, but the warm, soothing voice of the stranger had worked its magic, lulling E into a state of relaxation.

"Well then, let's do it on three."

E's heart pounded and he took a long breath before releasing it slowly.

"One..."

He placed his hands on the blindfold.

"Two..."

E could hear a slight tremor in his voice and tried to swallow it away.

"Three."

He pulled the blindfold off.

Oh.

E felt the blood drain from his face as he froze at the sight of the man in front of him. He was smiling, his eyes gleaming in the glow of the soft lighting overhead. He wore a snug, sky-blue shirt with two buttons open in a teasing display of skin. His hair was short with just a touch of product to keep it in shape, and E knew that, otherwise, it would swirl in unruly waves. It was the same strawberry-blond hair he'd thought of touching more times over the years than he'd like to admit.

Bile rose to his throat. He swallowed, doing his best to keep it down.

"Is this a joke?" E's words were a mere whisper, but he knew the man heard him, his face falling into a confused stare. "Did Latif put you up to this?"

"What? No." The man shook his head, frowning. "Who's Latif?"

"Uh-huh, right." E pushed off the table and stood abruptly enough for his chair to topple to the floor with a thud. With trembling fingers, he took out his glasses and shoved them back up his nose.

"Wait, where are you going?" The man shot to his feet to follow E.

"Home." E walked briskly, trying to manoeuvre between other tables without causing a scene. Finally, he reached the door and pushed it open, stumbling outside. The sharp, deep breath he took made him cough instead of calming him, but he kept walking, shoving his hands into the pockets of his jeans to keep them from shaking. Good thing he lived nearby; he'd be home soon.

Also by

The Blindfold Date:

MM Contemporary Romance (Pursuit of Love Series)

A new dating app. Rules: both parties sit at a table with blindfolds on. Each can ask three questions to the other. If they don't like the answers, they can leave. If both parties enjoy the conversation, they take the blindfold off. What can go wrong? Nothing. Unless after taking off the blindfold, you realise the other person is the last guy you expected to see.

This is exactly how Ernesto—an autistic video game programmer with a secret dominant streak, meets Brian—an easy-going ex-football player with a burgeoning desire to submit. And giving in to the demands of this lean, geeky Dom may be just what Brian needs.

A standalone MM book from the contemporary Pursuit of Love series. TW: D/S dynamics, mention of past abuse.

Get yours on Kindle Unlimited, eBook, or paperback: mybook.to/TheBlindfoldDate

The Flower Arrangement
MM Contemporary Romance Novella (Pursuit of Love Series)
Heartbroken after a bitter divorce, Brendan finds solace in running his beloved flower shop. Wary of being hurt again, he vows to think twice before jumping into a new relationship. Then he meets flamboyant hairstylist Hugh, a man with skilled hands and a cheeky smile who tests Brendan's resolve.

Hugh has at long last realised his dream of having his own salon, but the glow of his success is hampered by the shadow of his loneliness. When brawny, six-foot-three Brendan appears wielding a bouquet of exquisite flowers, Hugh feels that shadow begin to fade. Brendan's kind eyes, chequered shirt, and dad-next-door appeal dare Hugh to break his no-dating-clients rule.

Sparks fly as their desire for each other grows. Passion and laughter help heal old wounds, but only time will tell if it is enough to build a lasting relationship.

A story of second chances, idiots in love, and steamy jacuzzi scenes, this standalone MM novella is from the contemporary Pursuit of Love series.

Get yours on Kindle Unlimited, eBook, or paperback: mybook.to/TheFlower

The Sinner's Penance:

MM Contemporary Romance (Pursuit of Love Series)

He's supposed to stay hidden. His cassock is the perfect disguise. But he would never hide his carnal nature. Especially not when a handsome parishioner begs him to be punished for his dirty thoughts.

A standalone MM book 3 from Pursuit of Love series.

Get yours: mybook.to/SinnersPenance

Whispers in the Woods

MM Paranormal Novella (BPO Series)

When a gigantic forest creature saves Tomek from a falling tree, he feels an intense desire to know more about the young man the creature turns into. As Tomek and Robert's friendship blooms, the bigotry permeating society puts their relationship to question, while Tomek's heart fills with doubt and his head with denial about his sexuality. Will he be able to face his friend and admit his feelings? A new adult, queer tale of love in extraordinary times — full of emotion, reflection, and second chances.

Themes and tropes: pan + gay characters, shifter romance, fighting bigotry, friends to misunderstanding to lovers, Eastern European setting, MM, HEA.

Get yours on Kindle Unlimited, eBook, or paperback: mybook.to/WhispersInTheWoods

About Author

K. C. Carmine is a Polish-born writer, currently living in England. Her MA in English Philology and love of reading inspired her to start writing down the stories her imagination provided. As a member of the queer community, it is important to her that her writing reflects the diversity of voices around her. While she is a lover of romance, she also enjoys horror, paranormal and mystery stories. When she's not writing, she likes travelling, playing the guitar, video games, and reading.

To get my books on Amazon, please go to: author.to/KCCarmine

Find all my publications including short stories in anthologies and magazines go to https://kccarmine.carrd.co where you can also subscribe to my newsletter.

Follow/reach out to me on social media @kc_carmine